Padma Shri Pran

Maurice Horn, the editor of World Encyclopedia of Comics, has described cartoonist PRAN as Walt Disney of India.

Entertaining generation after generation, his comics have been constant companion of all the growing youngsters providing fun and amusement through his famous characters like CHACHA CHAUDHARY, SABU, SHRIMATIJI, PINKI, BILLOO, RAMAN etc. More than 600 of his titles are selling well in the market, and numerous comic strips are regularly appearing in various newspapers. His CHACHA CHAUDHARY comics had already been adapted for a TV Serial, and ran continuously for 600 episodes on a premier channel.

Travelling widely over the globe, he delivers lectures at various International Conferences. He has also been honoured with 'People of The Year Award' by Limca Book of Records for popularizing comics. His comic book 'United We Stand' was released in 1983 by the then Prime Minister Mrs. Indira Gandhi, and is still very popular among children.

Publisher

BILLOO AND GEMINI CIRCUS

EVEN WE'RE AGAINST THE USE OF ANIMALS IN THE CIRCUS.
EVERYONE IS OF THE SAME OPINION. HENCE I'VE SHUT IT.
WE OPPOSE THAT AS WELL.
YOU OPPOSE THIS AS WELL AS THAT.
WHAT DO YOU WANT ?
JUST THIS THAT YOU WON'T GO BACK.
AND THE CIRCUS ALSO SHOULDN'T SHUT DOWN.

HOW ?
WE'LL ENTERTAIN THE VIEWERS DRESSED UP LIKE ANIMALS.
WHAT DO YOU ALL SAY ?
ABSOLUTELY
BUT...?
NO IF NO BUT, YOU PREPARE FOR THE SHOW.
WE'LL DO OUR PREPARATIONS.
SOON...
WOW !!
CLAPPING !!

BILLOO AND FRIENDS DRESSED AS BEAR AND GORILLA SHOW THEIR TRICKS IN THE RING.
WONDERFUL !!
WONDERFUL !!
WOW !! GREAT !!
WOW ! THIS SHOW IS HOUSEFUL.
BILLOO AND HIS FRIENDS HAVE WORKED WONDERS.

LOTS OF MONEY COMING.
NOW YOU COUNT THIS MONEY IN THE JAIL.
WE'RE ARRESTING YOU FOR THE USE OF ANIMALS IN SPITE OF THE BAN.
BUT THEY WEREN'T ANIMALS, THEY...
GIVE YOUR EXPLANATION IN THE COURT.
SOB !! I WAS GOING BACK... BILLOO TRAPPED ME IN HIS WORDS... SOB!!

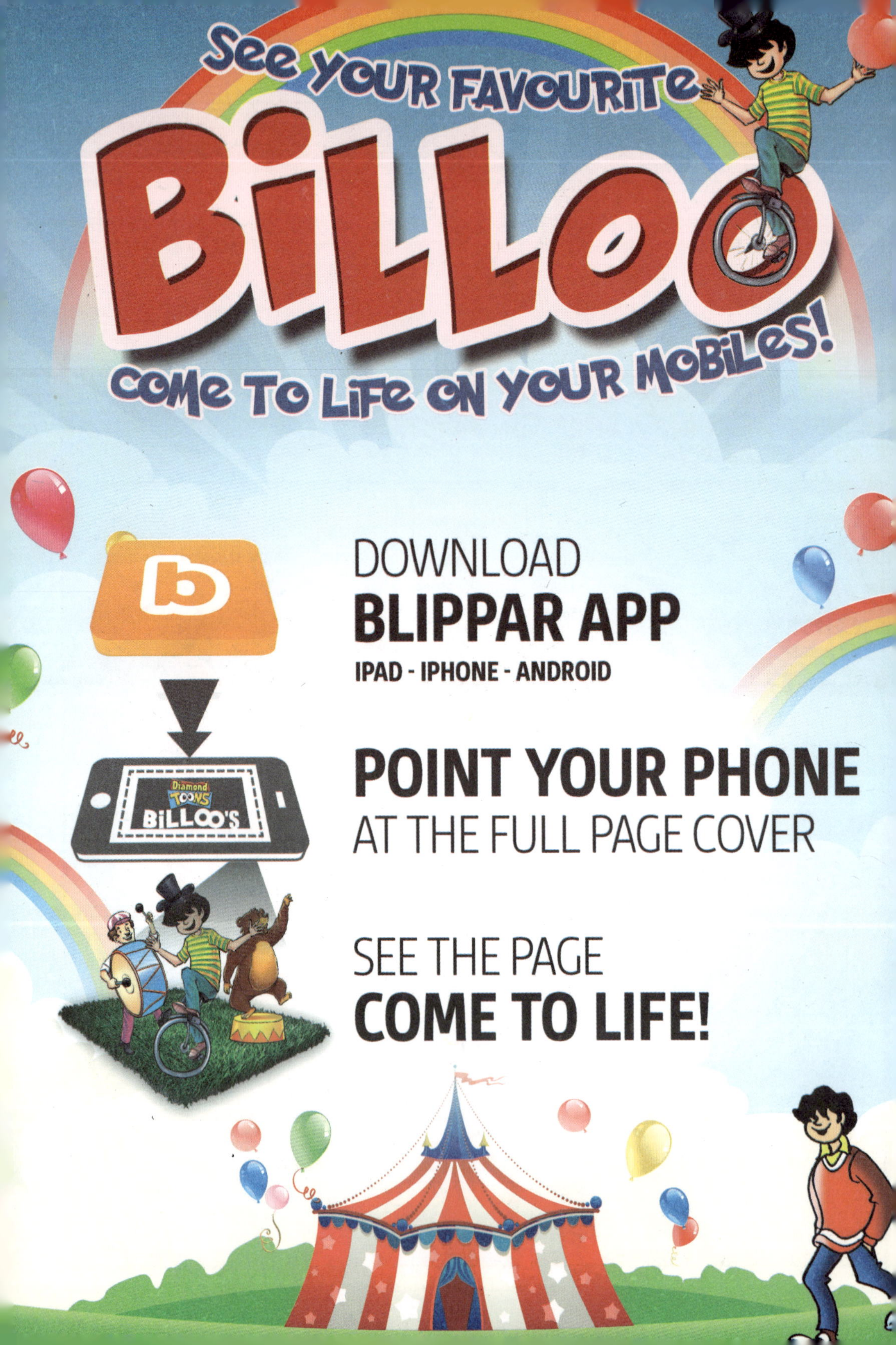
See your favourite
Billoo
come to life on your mobiles!
DOWNLOAD
BLIPPAR APP
IPAD - IPHONE - ANDROID
Diamond
TOONS
BILLOO'S
POINT YOUR PHONE
AT THE FULL PAGE COVER
SEE THE PAGE
COME TO LIFE!

PRAN'S
CHACHA CHAUDHARY
AND
TWIGGY

CHACHA CHAUDHARY AND TWIGGY

HELLO KIDS, LOOK WHAT I'VE BROUGHT YOU !
WOW, THIS LOOKS LIKE A BRAIN !
YES ! AND THEY ARE GREAT FOR YOUR HEALTH. AND REMEMBER, ONLY A HEALTHY BODY CAN BE HOME TO A SHARP MIND.
IS THAT WHY YOU ARE SO INTELLIGENT, CHACHA JI ?
AS A KID, I LIKED TO STUDY.
...BUT I HAD UNHEALTHY HABITS.
...AND WAS NOT VERY INTELLIGENT.

To learn more about Omega-3, visit www.walnuts.org

HOORAY! HOORAY!
LOOK! A THUG IS SNATCHING GOLD CHAIN FROM A LADY.
LET'S TEACH HIM A LESSON.
HEY, LOOK BEHIND YOU!
THE THUGS MIND IS DISTRACTED.

DHISHUM !
OWWW!
CHACHA CHAUDHARY ! YOU TRICKED ME.
HERE IS YOUR GOLD CHAIN.
FROM TODAY WE'LL ALSO HAVE CALIFORNIA WALNUTS, AND BE LIKE CHACHA JI !
Walnuts and Heart Health-Smart for the Heart
CALIFORNIA Walnuts
www.californiawalnuts.in
Contact for more nutrition facts & walnut recipes: www.californiawalnuts.in | walnuts@scs-group.com
Find us on: facebook.com/CaliforniaWalnuts.India twitter.com/CaWalnutsIndia

BECAUSE THAT'S THE SMART THING TO DO .

EAT CALIFORNIA WALNUTS EVERYDAY !!
CALIFORNIA Walnuts

RILLOO'S BOAT
BUDDY! WHAT ARE YOU MAKING?
MONU, IT'S A BOAT.
I'VE DISCOVERED A NEW WAY TO CONTACT PEOPLE OF FOREIGN NATIONS.
THE FLAG ON IT HAS MY PIC. SO WHEN THIS BOAT WILL GO TO FOREIGN LANDS, PEOPLE THERE WILL KNOW ME.

I'VE LEFT IT IN THE SEA.
SAILING ACROSS IT MIGHT REACH ANY COAST CHINESE, JAPANESE, SRI LANKAN, BURMESE...
BILLOO ! A WAVE HAS CAUGHT YOUR BOAT.
IT'S OVERTURNED.
I'LL GO AND PUT IT RIGHT.

OHHHH!
SAVE!
THANK GOD, I'VE REACHED SAFELY.
BILLOO! YOUR BOAT HAS REACHED THE SHORE. BUT YOU SHOULD BE HAPPY THAT THE JAPANESE TOURISTS ARE SEEING IT.

HI TINA !
HI BILLOO !
BILLOO
SWIMMING POOL
IS YOUR SWIMMING POOL READY ?
YES !
SEE !
WOW !

YOU'RE A LIAR BILLOO. YOU SAID IF I MAKE THE POOL, YOU'LL CONTRIBUTE IN IT.
I'VE COME FOR THAT.
HERE'S MY CONTRIBUTION A BOTTLE OF WATER.
FOR YOUR SWIMMING POOL.
!!
DON'T TALK RUBBISH BILLOO. HELP ME.
SEE ! I'VE KEPT A FEES FOR SWIMMING IN THE POOL.
BRING A FEW CUSTOMERS.

IT'S MY MORAL DUTY TO BRING CUSTOMERS FOR TINA'S POOL.
OH IT'S HOT!
CUSTOMER!
I'VE A SOLUTION FOR THIS HEAT. YOU CAN GO TO TINA'S SWIMMING POOL.
WE'RE VILLAGERS. HOW DO WE KNOW WHAT A SWIMMING POOL IS ?
IT'S LIKE THE POND YOU'VE GOT IN VILLAGES. HERE IT'S CALLED A SWIMMING POOL.
OK !
EXACTLY ! ITS FEES IS RS. 20 PER HOUR.
HERE, TAKE RS.100. THERE WILL BE 4 MORE ALONG ME.

BRING EVERYONE.
BRINGING.
TINA, TAKE RS.100, THE SWIMMING FEES OF YOUR FIRST FIVE CUSTOMERS.
WOW !!
THIS IS LIKE A GOOD FRIEND.
I'LL GO NOW. YOUR CUSTOMERS MUST BE ABOUT TO COME.
AFTER SOME TIME...
BILLOO! YOU RUINED MY SWIMMING POOL.
GRRRR !!
GRRRR !!

WHAT HAVE I DONE ??
I BROUGHT CUSTOMERS FOR YOU.
THESE ARE THE CUSTOMERS ?? GRRRR !!
!!
THIS POOL IS BETTER THAN OUR POND. EVEN THE BUFFALOES SEEM TO BE VERY HAPPY HERE.

BILLOO
AND
EXAMS
BUDDY ! THIS TIME THE EXAM IS VERY TOUGH. IT WAS BETTER LAST TIME.
HOW COME PAPPU ?
LAST TIME I GOT 10 MARKS LESS. HAD I GOT 10 MARKS MORE, IT WOULD'VE BECOME 100.
OK ! HOW MUCH DID YOU SCORE LAST TIME ?
ZERO !!

IF YOU PUT 10 MARKS BEFORE ZERO, IT BECOMES 100.
WORK HARD THIS TIME. YOU'LL GET GOOD MARKS.
IN THE EXAMINATION HALL...
ALL THE CHILDREN SHOULD TAKE THE ANSWER SHEET.
DON'T FORGET TO WRITE YOUR ROLL NO. ON IT.

THE EXAM IS FOR 3 HOURS.
AND YOUR TIME STARTS NOW.

TIME FINISH.
HOW WAS IT?
VERY FINE.
PAPPU YOURS ??
VERY NICE. JUST LEFT ONE QUESTION.
WHICH ONE ?

LAST.
WOW ! THAT MEANS YOU ATTEMPTED ALL OTHER QUESTIONS.
NO, I DIDN'T EVEN READ THE REST.
OH !
WHAT OH ?? DO YOU KNOW I WON'T FAIL AFTER THIS ALSO
HOW COME ?
I'VE WRITTEN IN THE ANSWER SHEET... DON'T DARE TO FAIL ME.

BILLOO
CRICKET BAT
I'M THE MOST IMPORTANT PLAYER OF THIS TEAM. I'M THE OPENER.
I AM OPENER.
OPENER.
BUDDY CAN YOU OPEN THIS COLD DRINK BOTTLE ?

I CAN'T OPEN IT ?
IF YOU CAN'T OPEN ITS LID HOW CAN I DO IT ?
YOU CAN BECAUSE YOU'RE AN OPENER... THAT MEANS ONE WHO CAN OPEN.
OH ! I'M NOT THAT OPENER. I'M THE OPENER OF CRICKET TEAM...ONE WHO BATS FIRST.
TODAY I'LL DO THE BATTING FIRST.
OH !
BAJRANGI PEHALWAN.
YES.

YOU'VE SNATCHED MY BAT ? IT'S NOT GOOD.
I DON'T NEED TO THINK WHAT IS GOOD OR BAD.
YOU DO THE BOWLING. I'LL DO THE BATTING.
GRRRR !
GRRRR !
OH !
THE BAT'S BROKEN.

YOU'VE BROKEN OUR EXPENSIVE BAT.
SO WHAT ? BRING ANOTHER BAT.
NO USE. THE OTHER ONE WILL ALSO BREAK.
SO ?
SOMETHING NEEDS TO BE DONE TO MAKE YOU BAT.
WHAT ?
YOU BRING THAT THICK TRUNK OF THE TREE. WE'LL MAKE A BAT OUT OF IT.
IT WON'T BREAK ON YOUR PLAYING ALSO.
GOOD IDEA.

I'LL BRING IT.
CUTTING A TREE IS AN OFFENCE. COME DOWN.
I'LL TAKE YOU TO THE PRISON.
SOB !!
YOU WERE RIGHT. WHEN DO PEOPLE LIKE YOU THINK OF RIGHT AND WRONG ?
COME NOW WE'LL PLAY WITHOUT ANY OBSTRUCTION.

BiLLOO RACE
BOW! BOW!
GOLDY! YOUR DOG BARKS VERY LOUDLY.
I'LL RECORD HIS SOUND.
BOW! BOW!

PANT! PANT!
ISN'T THIS CHANDU ?
WHY ARE YOU TORTURING YOURSELF CHANDU ?
MY DAD'S GOT MY NAME REGISTERED FOR A RACE COMPETITION FORCEFULLY.
I'M PRACTICING TO WIN THAT ONLY.
I'VE TO TAKE TWO ROUNDS OF THIS PARK. I CAN'T DO IT.
WHY NOT ?

GOLDY LEAVE YOUR DOG AFTER HIM.
BOW! BOW!
BOW!
ONE ROUND.
SECOND ROUND.
SEE HOW EASILY YOU TOOK TWO ROUNDS OF THE PARK.

NOW I'VE TO SEE HOW TO MAKE YOU WIN THE COMPETITION.
ON THE DAY OF THE RACE...
BUCK UP CHANDU.
RUN FAST CHANDU. FAST.
YOU'VE TO WIN THE RACE.
WHAT THE HELL ?? CHANDU CAN'T EVEN RUN PROPERLY.
I'LL DO SOMETHING TO MAKE CHANDU RUN.
WHAT ?

JUST WATCH.
RUN.
CHANDU FIRST.
THE RECORDING OF YOUR DOG'S BARKING ENABLED CHANDU TO WIN.
WOW!

BILLOO AKA TARZAN
JO JI! I WANT TO SEE YOU FOR A MINUTE.
BILLOO! DON'T COME HERE.
WHY?
MY DAD DOESN'T LIKE ANY BOY LOOKING AT HIS DAUGHTER. HE MIGHT SHOOT YOU.
BETTER WOULD BE . . . YOU COME BEHIND MY HOUSE AND GIVE A CRY LIKE TARZAN. I'LL COME IN THE WINDOW.

I MUST REACH EARLY.
JOJI'S HOUSE IS THERE.
HOO HO!
HOW ARE YOU BILLOO?
I'VE SEEN YOU. NOW MY DAY WOULD PASS WONDERFULLY.
ARE YOU THE ONE WHO GAVE THE CRY OF TARZAN?
YES!
SIGN THIS CONTRACT AND GET RS. 50,0001.

I'M DIRECTOR FLIP FLOP. I'M MAKING A FILM TARZAN. I HEARDYOUR CRY AND DECIDED YOU'LL PLAY THE ROLE OF TARZAN IN MY FILM.
SIT IN THE VAN. WE'RE GOING FOR OUTDOOR SHOOTING.
WHERE ARE WE GOING OUT TO ?
IN THE JUNGLE.
THE SCENE IS LION IS ABOUT TO KILL THE HEROINE. YOU'VE TO SAVE THE GIRL.
LION ?
DON'T WORRY. IT'S A TAME LION FROM A CIRCUS.

GRRRR!
SAVE ME!
CRACK !
OH!
BANG !
SQUEALLL!

MY LION'S BONE HAS BROKEN. YOU'LL PAY FOR THE TREATMENT.
OK, LET THE FILM RELEASE FIRST.
NEXT SCENE IS CITY DACOITS HAVE COME TO LOOT THE JUNGLE TREASURE...
TARZAN WILL FIGHT AND SAVE THE TREASURE FROM THEM.
DACOITS?
THEY'RE FAKE. NOTHING IS REAL IN FILMS.
HO ! HO ! TREASURE ! TAKE IT.
WE'LL BE MILLIONAIRES.
HO-HO !
?!

BANG !
YOU FOOL ! KNOCK AWAY THE DACOITS.
HOW ? THESE WILD VINES ARE WRAPPED AROUND ME.
CUT !
SCREAM !!

THIS SCENE ISN'T THERE IN THE SCRIPT.
BOSS! THAT GORILLA IS ORIGINAL.
OH GOD!
RUN!!
CAMERA AND OTHER EQUIPMENTS ARE LEFT OUT.
THIS FEAR IS ALWAYS THERE IN OUTDOOR SHOOTING.
I THINK YOU SHOULD DROP THE IDEA OF MAKING A FILM ON JUNGLE.

BiLLOO
MORNING WALK
AH!
WOW !
WONDERFUL !

YOUR STAMINA IS AMAZING BILLOO.
How?
HOW DO YOU REMAIN SO FIT ? TELL THE SECRET.
YOU'LL HAVE TO TELL THE SECRET.
JUST LIKE THAT.
OK.

I'LL REVEAL THE SECRET AT YOUR HOUSE.
BRING 1 KG OF MILK.
OK.
NOW.
PUT IT ON HEAT.
ADD LOTS OF CRUSHED CASHEWS AND ALMONDS IN IT.

PUT LITTLE HONEY.
NOW STIR IT WITH A SPOON.
KEEP ON STIRRING TILL THERE REMAINS ONE GLASS OF MILK.
DONE.

GOOD. NOW JUST MOVE ASIDE.
WATCH CARE FULLY.
POUR IT IN A GLASS.
DRINK IT.
SLURP ! SLURP !
SLURP ! SLURP !
!!
THIS IS THE SECRET OF MY STAMINA.
BANG!
UNDERSTOOD?